MARRYING THE OBCESSED CEO

IRIS WEST

CHAPTER ONE

Winona

"I'M GOING TO have a fantastic day! My colleagues will be wonderful people. There won't be anything I can't solve," I whisper to myself as I stroll towards my new job at Sanders Solutions, one of the fastest growing management consultancy firms in the country.

The nerves don't vanish, but visualizing a good day and repeating positive affirmations make me feel a little better. It helps that even though it's just gone seven, and it's late February, the sun is shining, and the air is pleasantly warm. Best of all, the cramps and migraine that had me bedridden yesterday are completely gone. If my period had started today, I would have had to call in sick on my first day, which would have sucked. I'm taking coming on yesterday as a good omen that this is going to be a successful day.

I need this job to be a success to prove to myself that moving back home to Blossom Ford isn't a complete failure. Otherwise, it'll be too hard to understand the fact that I couldn't stomach living away from home when I made a huge deal about living in Boston after college and graduate school, instead of bowing down to fate and doing what's expected of me, which is working for Blossom Ford matchmaking agency, like all the eldest girls of my family have done for generations.

Even though I missed home like crazy, I only left my job of one year at a large Boston firm when I found something better at home. My post at Sanders Solution is initially for a four-month maternity cover and the company is not as large as the top firm I worked for in Boston, still it comes with the possibility of permanent employment if I prove myself and as assistant to the CEO, it's a promotion with better pay and performance bonuses.

I have my own apartment, which means I'm independent. Popping home nearly every day and sleeping over at weekends doesn't count as being too reliant on my family's company, it just shows I missed them when I lived in away.

Besides, in a couple of weeks, Mom and Dad are going to visit one of my uncles who's been ill for a while. I'm learning to manage the agency so I can resolve any issues if anything urgent comes up. That's easier done at home. If I need any files, I can slip into the agency's small office, which is next to our house.

If only I could get my love life or lack of sorted, I'd be on cloud nine. Honestly, what twenty-five-year-old girl hasn't had at least one serious relationship? The type where one considers marriage or living together. The feeling that I'm the only one just won't go away. It's not that I'm not trying. The last three years I've been on countless dates, but they led nowhere. The men are too tall or short, too talkative or quiet, etc. My brain and body have come up with many excuses for why my dates weren't worth second chances.

And it's all because of one man. My one-night stand of three years ago. I don't even know his name, so I call him Lothario, but I remember his mesmerizing cerulean blue eyes and the feel of his beard and calloused hands on my feverish skin. I can't forget his chiseled face because I dream of him almost every night. Vivid dreams that leave me panting, my pussy wet, when I wake up.

I don't know what to do to forget him. I definitely can't forget how gentle he became when he realized I was a virgin and the tender way he wiped the blood off my thighs afterward.

My friends and I had flown to New York City from Boston for a weekend trip and when we hit the bar, they dared me to lose my virginity. They'd tried the dare countless times before, but I'd never given in. Yet, that night, from the moment I saw Lothario, I was powerless against the lust that surged within me.

I greet the two security men at the entrance of the building that houses my new company. Fishing out my badge, I let myself in and take the elevator to the top of the building. Sanders Solutions occupies the top two floors, with the executives being on the fifteenth floor.

I pass quiet desks and offices until I reach my room. Light peeps through the door of the CEO's office and my lips quirk up.

It's not even half past seven. I feel sorry for his private life, but I love his dedication to work. No wonder he made the company he started in college into the giant force it is today in only fifteen years.

Julian Sanders was a lost, hurting young man when I tried to comfort him seventeen years ago. Aged eight, I'd been mad at having to attend a funeral where I was the only child. I was bored and was exploring the Sanders' small house when I stumbled on him inside his deceased grandad's bedroom. He'd looked old to me, but now I know he must have been around twenty-three, and although I couldn't really explain the depth of the feelings his naked eyes conveyed, I'd felt like he was the saddest person in the world.

When I told Mom the name of the company I'd be working for, she'd explained it belonged to Mr. Sanders' grandson. I can't wait to meet him.

Few people had a good word to say about him during the two years he lived in Blossom Ford when he was a teenager. He'd dropped out of high school and run off to a big city and only visited his grandad on

Christmas day.

But now he was back in town as a highly respected owner of a business that generated billions in revenue and created jobs in town.

I slide out of my sneakers and slip into my favorite work heels. I switch on my laptop and once again go over the notes from Mr. Sanders' assistant, whom I was supposed to shadow for a few days. She went into early labor but left a comprehensive itemized list of instructions.

Eager to start my day and meet my new boss, I head to his office.

"Come in," a deep voice calls out in reply to my knock.

A shiver runs up my spine. I know that voice. Intimately. It whispers to me in the dark of night and sometimes when I'm showering.

I shake my head. Remind myself this is a place of work. Lothario and the delicious things he does to me don't belong here.

I square my shoulder, lift my chin and open the door.

Julian Sanders is staring at one of the laptops on his massive desk. He looks up and the greeting at the tip of my mouth vanishes.

Familiar blue eyes under thick chestnut brows root me to the spot. It's Lothario! His hair is cropped shorter at the sides and his beard is thicker, but his wide forehead and crooked nose remain the same. A dark tailored suit jacket encases his broad shoulders, just like that fateful night in New York City three years ago.

I blink, twice. Lothario is still watching me. It's hard to tell if he remembers me, but the fire in his eyes is unmistakable. It makes me feel owned, as if he branded me. Heat suffuses my whole body and face. Desire stirs my lower body. A part of my mind wonders if that look is the reason I could not forget this man.

The sound of voices, probably from the cleaning crew, brings me back to my senses.

I remind myself that I need this job. The precious pleasure this man brought me belongs only in the deepest recesses of my mind. The only thing I can do in this situation is to behave as the professional I'm supposed to be. Because Lothario is my boss, and that means nothing can ever happen between the two of us.

Once again, I set my shoulders back and lift my chin. My mouth is dry, so I clear my throat and march forward.

"Good morning Mr. Sanders. It's a pleasure to meet you. I'm Winona Smith, your temporary assistant." I stretch my hand out, glad I learned to fake a smile and a firm voice like a pro.

CHAPTER TWO

Julian

I STAND UP and clutch Winona's, not Temptress as I call her in my dreams, hand. It's soft and plump, just like her. Her nails are red gold and clipped short like they were that night.

I hold on a little longer than necessary but when I speak, my voice hides the bottomless cauldron of frustration and raging need this beauty has caused inside me since I met her three long years ago. I tried meeting the most beautiful women on the planet and working myself to exhaustion in order to forget her, to no avail. She's an obsession I can't rid myself of.

"Julian Sanders. The pleasure is all mine."

This expression has never made more sense than it does at this moment. My mind is stuck on the word mine like a broken record. And it's been playing since the moment I looked up and saw her.

I've been dreaming of this woman practically every time I close my eyes. Her peaches and cream scent, the taste of her rosy lips, the way her tightly curled hair feels in my hands, and the screams she makes when she comes are imprinted in my mind. So is the smile that lights up her champagne hued eyes and the so right way she felt as she slept in my arms.

She's still as alluring and sexy as I remember. But there's a deeper level of maturity and confidence about her eyes that wasn't there before. I've felt lust and a sense of belonging for my temptress, but now respect and pride warm my heart at the way she's holding herself straight, her chin jutting forward.

I spied the shock on her face when she saw me. She recognized me. I don't know how much of an impression I made in her life, but it's clear she hasn't forgotten our heated night of passion. The blush on her cheeks may be a sign of embarrassment, however, the heat in her eyes tells me she still finds me attractive.

That and the determination in her posture calm the urge to splay her over my desk and make love to her body until she's senseless with pleasure.

I am not an animal, no matter how I feel like one right now.

The cool tone of her voice reminds me of my responsibilities as her employer. I motion for her to sit and silently say a thank you because I'm wearing my suit jacket so she's not embarrassed by my hard on.

"Did you bring yourself up to speed with the status of our most pressing projects and what needs organizing the next couple of days?" My voice is rougher than usual, yet there's nothing I can do about it. It's taken everything in me to control myself and pretend this is the first time we're meeting and my hands are not dying to touch her.

I don't give a fuck what people think of me, but I want her to like me. For now, I'll go along with pretending like we're strangers, like she apparently wants.

"Yes. I've organized the notes for the two conference calls this afternoon. I'll contact our new client and make an initial assessment on the implementation of the new audible software."

We spend the next half-hour going over the most complex of our current projects.

"I'm impressed. Lori was on point when she said you're going to be one of her best hires. Welcome to Sanders Solutions."

My assistant wasn't easily impressed, but she raved about Winona's analytical, planning and problem-solving skills. I'd been a little skeptical because although Winona earned her MBA summa cum laude, her working experience was limited to a year of full-time employment, albeit with one of the best management consultancy firms in the world, and internships she'd taken over the summer breaks of her college life. Thank God I trusted my employees' judgement and Winona was hired.

"Thank you. Would you like a cup of coffee?"

It's a perfectly normal question, and her voice is only projecting politeness. Why is my mind suddenly filled with images of the flirty way she'd approached me at the bar in New York?

I don't need a drink, but I want to see her walk toward me again, so I nod and watch the sway of her hips until she leaves the room.

I erupt out of my chair and face the stretch of mountain visible through the floor to ceiling glass walls. It's a breathtaking view, but today, there's too much chaos in my mind for me to enjoy it.

Fucking hell!

I searched for Winona after she snuck out of our hotel room. I returned to the bar I met her again and again, hoping to see her there. Every time I saw a curvy, caramel skinned woman, my hopes would rise only to be crushed when they turned out to be someone else. There's no way I can accept just being colleagues with her.

I won't break my rule of not getting involved with the staff. I solve problems for a living. Somehow, I'll have to solve this one too.

I shove my hands into my trousers' pockets and pace across the length of the office. In the last couple of months, I've been thinking about creating a foundation to fund facilities that provide respite care for parents of disabled children. It's an idea that was put forward by one of my employees who has a disabled nephew. He'd been passionate when he talked about the toll caring for the disabled child took, but his field of expertise lies in computer programming.

Maybe it's something Winona can manage when Lori returns from maternity leave. She'd shown an interest in staying with the company once her initial four months were up.

I stop myself.

What the hell am I doing?

I don't even know what the woman wants. Over the years, I've wondered about why she scurried out of the hotel suite without so much as a goodbye. She'd enjoyed the sex as much as I did. Although she'd been experienced at flirting and foreplay, the red stains on her thighs and sheet proved this wasn't something she did often.

A lot of reasons popped into my mind. Ultimately, I used my experience to conclude that although she'd loved the sex, our time together hadn't meant more to her than the desire to scratch an itch. Although unexpected, it had meant so much more to me.

Before Winona, sex was a way to blow off steam from a hard day of work. I made sure my partners knew it. The idea of having the same sexual partner for a long period was burdensome.

Now, I want Winona in my life. If she's married, I won't touch her. But anything else, I'm ready to deal with. I'll do whatever it takes to make her realize she'll have a better life with me.

CHAPTER THREE

Winona

IT'S MY THIRD day at Sanders Solutions and I'm exhausted. I've been attending meetings, introducing myself to clients and working on some complex projects the company has taken on, as well as getting to know the other staff members. It's better this way because during work hours, I have very little time to think about how Lothario has only become hotter and harder to resist.

He insists I call him Julian. Since everyone seems to be on a first name basis, I cave in.

A problem arises with one of our clients, so we stay later than usual. There are about ten of us in the meeting room and we eat takeout pizza as we work to clear the issue. By half-past nine, most of the work is done and only Julian and I remain to tidy things up.

"We're done. I'll give you a lift." Julian stands up and rotates his shoulders.

"You don't have to. It's late, you should get some rest."

He fixes those irresistible blues on me. "I think you have the wrong idea about me."

His tone is light. His lips quirk up just the tiniest bit as he affects a hurt expression.

I've seen his sexy, dominant, hard-working, serious and generous sides, but this is the first time he's shown his playful side in front of me. Even when we flirted in the past, she was guarded.

My lips lift in response.

"I took Lori home occasionally. It's late. I've seen you walk in the morning, so I know you are not driving. Is it wrong of me to want to do the gentlemanly thing and offer you a ride?"

Now I feel petty.

"I'll get my things."

We both grab our stuff and head for the elevator. The moment the door closes on us, I become super aware of Julian. His scent, a combination of musk and something that's just him, reaches my nostrils. It's like a drug to me. Suddenly, the taste of his kiss and the seductive warmth of his touch against my skin rush to my mind and I'm reminded of the reason I didn't want to take him up on his offer of a ride. Being alone with him in such a close space is sweet torture. I want to touch him but can't.

In his car, I sink into the luxurious passenger seat and almost purr at how comfortable I feel. He asks for my address and heads off the minute I finish speaking.

"How did you start your business?" I ask. I'm curious, but I also need something to focus on other than the confident way his powerful hands move over the wheel.

"Through sheer desperation." He glances at me.

I'm even more curious now.

"I'm a high school dropout. I blamed my unhappy childhood for everything that went wrong in my life and wanted to get back at the world that didn't seem to give a damn about me. I wasted my late teens and early twenties drinking away every penny I made."

He stops at a red light and stares at me. I gaze back at him, surprised by his expression and the way he's willing to open himself up. His employees admire and respect him, but they all seem to have the impression that he keeps his private life to himself. He was never this open three years ago.

"Then one day I was truly alone. I realized I had to change."

He gives me a lopsided grin.

"A little angel told me I was a good boy."

"An angel?"

"A know it all of a little girl. She gave me a rainbow lollipop too. Said it'd give me a little happiness."

I choke.

"Okay?" Concern lines his face.

I nod. I don't know whether to tell him I'm that little girl. This is so messed up. I want to tell him I'm touched he remembers something that happened all those years ago and that my words actually comforted him. But the one-night incident, the best and worst decision of my life, makes me unsure.

Julian pulls up outside my block of flats, kills the engine, and turns to me.

"Did the lollipop bring you happiness?" He doesn't seem like the type of man to believe in childish things like that.

"She was at my grandad's funeral. He and my mom didn't get along, so I didn't meet him until I was fourteen, when he had to take me in. I was dealing with my own demons, and he wasn't much of a talker. Suddenly facing a troubled teen couldn't have been easy for him, but I didn't see that."

"It must have been hard for both of you," I add. I was too young to be aware of what was happening, but I heard scraps from adults' conversation about how tough and sad things were for the Sanders.

"She, my little angel, said she'd overheard grandad say he hoped I'd realize I was a good boy and would do something with my life, when I asked how she knew what I was like."

"She was right. You are a good man. You give so much back to society, and you genuinely care about your staff."

Something shifts in his eyes. He cocks his head.

There's a hint of a smile in his eyes.

"That's not what it looked like when you refused a lift."

I blink at him. "It's only a five-minute drive. I wanted to save you the trouble."

Julian is watching me so closely, as if he's trying to figure me out.

"What did you do after your encounter with your little angel?"

"I took the GED, went to college, and worked my ass off. When things got tough, I looked at the lollipop and reminded myself Grandad had believed in me. I started the company my second year of college and grew it little by little."

"You must be proud of yourself. Your grandad would be proud of you too."

A tinge of pink shades his cheeks. This time, when he smiles, his eyes crinkle and I can see his even white teeth.

"I hope so."

Warmth spreads through me and I know it's going to be almost impossible stopping the journey from lust to more. In the last three days, I've fallen a little in love with Julian's drive and passion for his work, but seeing this humble side of him just took that to another level.

"Thanks for the lift. I'll see you tomorrow."

He waits until I'm inside the building before he drives off.

CHAPTER FOUR

Julian

I WAKE UP to a cry of pleasure and a wet, rock-hard cock. I grab onto it and stroke up and down, spreading the moisture at the tip so my hand glides over the sensitive skin. My ministrations are no-where near as good as Winona's three years ago, and the way she pleasures me in my dreams, but they'll do. After only five pumps I grunt at the feel-good sensation as come spurts onto my stomach and navel, where the word Temptress is inked in small black letters.

Dreaming about that night again and again has been both pleasurable and painful. Seeing my temptress every day, working with her, is making me long for her even more.

I'm glad it's Monday. The weekend felt empty without her. I thought about making up an excuse so she'd have to work some of the weekend, but remembering the sight of her yawning at the end of a hectic Friday stopped me.

Now and then, I'd look up, expecting her to march into my office with a cup of coffee. Even though we've been working together for only a week, it felt weird not seeing her at her desk, poring over something on her laptop. I've always worked weekends and loved it when I was the only soul there, just as much as I loved being at the office with my employees working in the background.

For the first time, on a weekend, being alone at the office felt lonely.

It was a relief when seven o'clock came and I headed for the dojo and released a lot of my pent up frustration punching, striking and kicking the boxing bag.

I slide out of the massive bed and strip the sheets. As I shower and get ready for work, I think about the plan I've devised to seduce my temptress.

The file that HR has about her suggests she's single. She seems to be comfortable pretending our one night together never happened, therefore for now, I'll carry on going along with it.

When I think about the night I told Winona my story, I'm filled with embarrassment. That was the first time I'd ever told anyone about the dark and painful days of my teenage years. I've given interviews to magazines about the rise of Sanders Solutions, but I always keep the personal stuff about Grandad, Mom, and the troubled teenager I was out of it. Saying I had a tough childhood was all I'd ever been willing to say.

I wanted Winona to know where I come from. I was also hoping that opening up about myself will make her want to do the same. Already, the caution in her eyes has diminished. I'm seeing more of the friendly and flirty personality she showed that night three years ago.

Being a caring and friendly employer while creating as many opportunities as possible to spend time with her has made Winona trust me a little and is giving us a chance to get to know each other.

My house is under the mountains of Blossom Ford, so the drive to work only takes ten minutes. It's seven o'clock when I walk into the office, excited for the challenges work will bring and the anticipation of spending time with Winona.

Half an hour later, I sense her arrival. Even though she comes into the office quietly, I always know when she's around. Once she changes out of her sneakers, the staccato clicks of her heels let me know when she's approaching my office.

I must look silly with the huge grin on my face, but I don't give a toss. Work has never been so sweet.

***

WINONA AND I have been working in my office for a couple of hours when an employee brings a food delivery bag.

"Let's take a break," I say after the staff member leaves.

I make space on the table for the food.

"Do you need some time alone?" I ask when she gathers up her laptop and tablet.

"We've eaten together when we worked over lunch with the teams. Since it's just the two of us, I thought you might prefer to eat alone."

"I honestly think talking about something other than work for a few minutes while eating generates more creativity once the break is over. Maybe bonding over food helps people work together better. There's more than enough food for us, too."

Winona chuckles. Just listening to the sound makes me feel good.
Her hair is up and she's wearing one of her belted jumpsuits, a red one this time, that flows over her curves and shows some of the skin above her cleavage. I smash that train of thought because it leads to a dangerous path.

"I think the creativity may have something to do with being grateful for a free lunch, the overtime pay and the excellent working conditions. They are great motivators for productivity."

"You got me." I watch her bite into a sandwich and focus on eating. "How was your weekend?" I ask when I finish a sandwich.

"Mom runs a small business. She's traveling in a

couple of weeks, so she's been showing me the ropes so I can deal with any urgent queries that come up while she's away. I spent the weekend and last weekend working on the business on my own to make sure I don't get any surprises. I prefer to learn by practice."

"How did it go?"

"It was frustrating." She sighs. "Mom is a college graduate, but she runs the business in an old-fashioned way. She'd have more clients and be much more successful if she only changed a few things. It wouldn't take much too."

As I listen to her ideas for improving her mom's business and give a few of my own, I realize I love this side of her. The way she becomes animated when she's talking about something she's interested in.

CHAPTER FIVE

Winona

I PLACE THE bar of chocolate Ebony, the only other staff member younger than me, gifted as my one-month employment anniversary on my desk. She's so friendly and reminds me of my best friend, Ella.

My cell vibrates. It's Shanay, Granny's caregiver. I'm about to clock out. Why is she calling? Heart sinking, I pick up.

"I'm so sorry Winona. Your granny took a nap an hour ago. I went to check in on her, but she wasn't there. I'm so sorry, but I can't find her," she sobs.

The cell slips through my fingers. I'm numb everywhere. My legs give way and I drop onto the chair behind me.

"What's the matter?" Julian asks as he comes toward me.

My mind is blank.

He picks up the phone, listens for a while.

"We'll call back in a minute," he says.

He puts his hands on my shoulders. I focus on him.

"I have a family emergency. I need to go."

"I'll give you a ride."

I call Shanay back as we head to the elevator. She's already contacted the police.

"Stay there and keep the house line open, in case someone calls with news. I'll check the places she might have gone."

"I'll call the diner. She might have gone there. Thank God the weather's warm. Should I call your mom and dad?"

"No!"

"Where to?"

"The main part of town. There's a park near Jackson's Diner she loves to visit. She likes the diner, too."

I blink back tears. Granny has gone missing a few times when I was away in college, but Mom and Dad always told me after they'd found her. Every time it happened, they must have felt as distressed as I am right now.

I look left and right, scanning the pavements. Mom and Dad have not found Granny on this side of town, but I might as well eliminate the area while I'm passing through.

Something warm touches my hand. It's Julian's

hand. I've been clutching my bag so hard, my knuckles have turned white. I place my hands flat against the bag, and Julian threads his fingers through mine.

I squeeze his hand, grateful.

"Where else might she have gone?"

I know all the places she's been found before, but in my mind I go over the list Mom left of likely places Granny might go to.

"The cinema and the elementary school. The point too, she likes the river."

"Tell me about your granny. What's she like?"

I smile. Granny's one of my favorite people. Maybe because she's always lived with us, in some ways, I'm closer to her than Mom.

After I tell Julian about her physical appearance, I talk about learning to cook from her and going berry picking together. When I was little, if I wasn't playing with Ella, I was hanging out with Granny. Even now, when her memory of the latest part of her life is fading, she still remembers most of those moments.

She's not at Jackson's Diner or the park. Neither is she at Raven's hairdresser. We still have more places to check, and I know an officer is looking for her and word has gotten round, which means the townsfolk will keep an eye out for her, but it's hard to keep the panic away.

I'm debating where to go next when Julian stops at a traffic light and my cell rings.

"She's at the grocery store. Lucy just called," the

caregiver says when I answer the phone.

I wipe away a tear and look at Julian. His face is a study in concern.

"The grocery store over there. The store owner's daughter just called."

I sprint out of the car when Julian stops the car. Granny is sitting comfortably inside the shop drinking lemonade. When I wrap her tightly in my arms, she pushes my hands away.

"What's this fuss about? I only popped out to get some popsicles. They are out of stock of my favorite brand. I'm tired. Let's go home."

I thank Lucy and walk out with Granny.

Maybe she's just realized Julian is with us because when he opens the car door for her, she freezes. She stares up at him for ages and I'm about to guide her into the car when her gaze shifts to me.

"He's a little too much like his granddaddy, but I like him," she says, then gets into the car.

I am mortified. How could Granny play cupid at a moment like this? In front of Julian, of all people. That I agree with her is irrelevant right now.

"Sometimes Granny–"

"I'm glad she approves of me," Julian cuts me off.

I decide to deal with that later and get into the back of the car with Granny.

"Your Granny's house or your apartment?" Julian asks.

"Granny's. My parents are away. I'm staying there

for the time being."

I call the caregiver, thank her and tell the poor woman to go home.

CHAPTER SIX

Julian

WINONA'S GRANNY'S HOUSE has changed little in the last twenty years. I remember coming here a few times to run errands for Grandad. It must have been about a year before Winona was born. A thought suddenly occurs to me. What if the reason Winona left without saying goodbye that night is my age? I make sure I'm fit and healthy, but she's young. What if our age gap is a deal breaker for anything more than a one-night stand?

I get up from the sofa and stroll towards a vast frame with a collage of family photos. I recognize Winona's parents. Although I didn't know their identity, they were at Grandad's funeral. Almost in all the photos, Winona's making a funny face. I'm not even surprised when I find that cute. My brain is obsessed with anything she does.

A couple of pictures catch my attention. My angel, the little girl that spoke with me at the funeral, is in them, with Winona's granny in one and Winona's parents in another. I look back at the other photos.

Winona is my little angel!

I don't know why she didn't mention it when I told her about my past. The only way I'll know the answer is by asking, so I keep busy as I wait for her to settle her granny.

I head out of the living room and go searching for the kitchen. We left the office just after six and it's now half-past eight. Winona's probably hungry. I want to make a cup of tea or coffee; it might help if she's still in shock. Don't people on TV use hot drinks to calm people?

I'm more of a scotch type man whenever I need to calm down, and so were Mom and Grandad. I find the kettle, fill it up and switch it on. When I stand in front of the refrigerator, I'm suddenly struck with unfamiliar nerves. What if Winona's parents object to having a stranger rummaging in their refrigerator?

I shake the nerves off. I doubt Winona wants takeout. Her granny would sometimes take us food. This house seems like the type that might always have something to eat lying around. Sure enough, there's some stew inside.

I warm some up, make two cups of coffee and set them on the table, just as footsteps sound on the stairs.

"I'm in the kitchen."

"Oh," Winona says when she sees me. "I was gone so long, I thought you'd left. I was going to call."

There are tear tracks on her cheeks. I want to sit with her on my lap, pat her back and say I don't know what to comfort her. Instead, I fold my arms over my chest to stop myself from putting thought into action. We need to talk first.

"I'm going to wash my face."

Back in the kitchen, she gulps her food. "Thanks for this. I was craving Granny's food. She made it yesterday."

"It's good. I never let on, but I used to love this whenever your granny gave some to Grandad."

She's silent, her champagne eyes downcast.

"We can talk another day. I'll do the dishes and go."

She finishes her food and grabs her coffee.

"I'm a little tired, but I want to talk. What happened with Granny made me realize I've been running away from some things and it's time to stop."

"What do you mean?" It sounds like she's talking about more than us.

"Kids used to call Granny a witch. And later Mom. I think that's when I began thinking I wanted nothing to do with the matchmaking agency or Granny and Mom's knowledge of medicinal herbs."

She smiles.

"I don't know if you're aware, but our matchmaking agency has only ever been run by the daughters of our family. I hated the expectation that as the only daughter, that's what I'd do. So, I did something else and am good at it." She takes another deep breath.

"But I've loved helping Mom run the agency the last few weeks. I want to modernize it, run it my way. And I want to spend more time with Granny while she still recognizes me. I think Mom wants that too. We can both do that if I run the agency."

I nod.

"You're not surprised?"

"When you talked about your mom's small business, I kind of figured you were in love with it."

"I'll complete my contract."

I want this woman permanently in my life. I want to marry her.

"I'm sorry I pretended not to know you. That first day at the office, I panicked. I didn't know how you'd feel about us working together. I also wasn't sure if you remembered me. Pretending we'd never met seemed to be the best option."

"I remember every single moment."

She blushes. Her tongue pops out and wets her lips. My eyes track the movement.

"Me too. It was the most amazing night of my life. You looked very successful; I didn't think you'd want to date me-"

"I dreamed about you for three years. I searched too."

"I went back to Boston straight away." Her fingers

play with the side of her cup. “Usually, I would have tried to persuade you, but even before we went to the hotel room, you made it clear you weren’t interested in relationships.”

Before I fell asleep, I should have made it clear to her that in the time we were together, I changed my mind.

“That was before you. I’m sorry I didn’t clarify that before I fell asleep. Since that night, you’re the only woman I’ve thought of. I want you in my life.” I curse myself for my choice of words. Why the hell did I find it hard to talk about my personal feelings? Should I have asked her out? Like on a date?

“You don’t get involved with your staff.”

Is she flirting with me? My eyes narrow.

Winona smiles. I lean back on the chair.

“You’re planning to leave in three months’ time. Even if you weren’t, I had a plan.”

I tell her about my solution, and she grins.

“What did you mean by wanting me in your life?”

There’s desire in her eyes, but there’s something else too. In the four weeks since she began working for me, I’ve become familiar with the expressions that flit across her face.

“I already know I want to spend the rest of my life with you. I understand you might not feel the same yet. Will you go out with me? To find out?”

“The day I finish my contract.”

We stare at each other. I’ve never met a woman with such a perfect combination of sass and sweetness. My heart stutters and I know I love her. I'm willing to wait for her.

"I saw your family photos; I know you're my little angel."

"Sorry about that. I wanted to tell you; I just wasn't sure how because of the one-night stand issue."

"Promise me one thing."

"What is it?"

"Let's be open with each other about things that affect our relationship."

"Deal."

CHAPTER SEVEN

Winona

IT'S MY LAST day at Sanders Solutions. I've said my goodbyes. It's one minute to seven o'clock, and it's Friday. It's so quiet, I think Julian and I are the only ones who haven't left.

My office phone rings.

"Miss Smith, come into my office, please."

I frown. As I walk into his room, the minute hand strikes 12. Officially, I'm no longer Julian's employee.

"Lock the door."

I shiver at the tone of his voice. I lock the door and look back at Julian. He's out of the chair and marches straight to me.

"I'm going to worship you tonight, Temptress," he whispers against my mouth.

I wrap my arms around the nape of his neck and

hold on for dear life as he devours my mouth in a wet kiss that makes my knees weak.

I'm grateful when he picks me up, still kissing me. I hook my legs around him and kiss him back, abandoning myself to the pleasure coursing through my mind.

He meanders to the desk and lowers me onto it. I open my legs and watch him step into the space between them.

"I love how thick your beard is."

I slide my hands up the sides of his face, delighting in the sensation of the bristles against my palms. Julian turns his head, captures one of my fingers into his mouth, and sucks on it. My core clenches.

I snake one arm round his neck and pull him down, wanting his mouth on me again. He nibbles my lower lip, draws it into his mouth with just the right amount of pressure.

He palms my breasts through the fabric of my dress, then squeezes them.

I moan into his mouth.

When I come up for air, Julian presses tiny kisses over my eyes, nose and jaw while his hands glide over my belly and thighs.

"I want to see you, Temptress."

The roughness in his voice is such a turn on.

I place my hand on the zip of my dress, but he removes it.

He drags the zip past my thighs until both sides of

the dress fall open.

"I love this dress."

I lift so he can pull the dress from under me.

He removes my strapless bra and knickers and stares at me, eyes darkening.

"Lie down." He shoves the papers on his desk away.

I lean back, feeling like a cat. The only other time I've ever been this exposed was the night we spent together. The heat in his eyes makes me feel wanton and takes away my shyness.

"Open your legs. I want to see the dark pink of your pussy. Stretch your arms above you."

He watches me like he's imagining the things he wants to do to me. My whole body is on fire. My chest rises with my quick breaths.

Julian strips slowly, his eyes roving over me. His large cock jerks against his belly. My eyes widen at how aroused he is.

"You got a tattoo?" It wasn't there before.

"Keep your hands up. Don't move."

"I want to see it."

He moves his cock away and I see it. It's so sexy, moistures seeps out of me. I bite my lip.

"You're my temptress, Winona. That's what I called you, the three years I didn't know your name."

Tears fill my eyes. Julian rubs his nose up the slit of my pussy and I cry out, tears forgotten.

"I missed this scent." He kisses the inside of my thighs, then kneels on the floor and places my legs on his shoulders.

He opens me wide, licks my clit. He blows on it like he's playing with a favorite toy, takes it into his mouth and sucks repeatedly until my whole body is arched off the table and I'm screaming with pleasure.

When I'm limp, he stands up, bends over and kisses me.

His cock is wet and hot against my belly. I push him off me and stand up. I take him in both of my hands and stroke him. Without letting go, I kneel and glide my mouth down on him.

He grunts, wraps his hand round my neck.

"That's it Temptress, just like that."

I drop one hand to his balls, play with them, and smile when he grunts again. I love hearing those growly sounds.

Just when I think he's getting closer to orgasm, he pulls back. I moan.

"Next time, I want to come inside you."

"That's what you said last time. I want you to come in my mouth like I did."

Indecision flickers across his face.

I wrap my hand round him and take him into my mouth again. Each time I suck up and down his cock, my hand follows.

Soon, Julian's thrusting against my mouth, groaning hoarsely, and my heart soars when he loses control and shouts my name, his come spurting down my throat.

He carries me to the couch, and we lie down with my back against his front. I must have fallen asleep because when I wake up, Julian's stroking my breasts. He plays with my nipples until they are as hard as pebbles. Arrows of pleasure shoot through my body.

I reach my hand back around his neck as he nibbles on mine. He caresses the side of my hip and angles my butt. When he penetrates me, the burn is a heady mixture of pleasure and pain.

"You're so fucking tight, Temptress."

"I love your nickname for me."

He chokes on a laugh when I move back against him.

"You okay?"

"Will you move already? I've waited over three years for this."

He laughs again.

Then he adjusts us so that one of his arms stretches out alongside mine. He intertwines our hands.

He drives into me, lazily at first, then faster, his free hand holding me in place for him.

"I love you, Winona Smith." He punctuates each word with a powerful thrust.

My body is a mass of bliss. I just make out his words.

"Who's your man, Temptress?"

I push back against him. I'm so close to orgasm; it's all I can think about.

"Say it! Who's your man?"

"Julian! You're my man!"

He rubs my clit, and I explode, bucking against him.

Julian screams against my neck and holds me tightly as his hot come shoots up my channel.

“I love you too,” I say when I can speak.

EPILOGUE

Julian

Three Months Later

IT'S MY WEDDING day. I've never been as nervous as I am today. I'm convinced Winona will not turn up. The feeling is killing me.

I wait for her at the altar. The whole town seems to be packed inside the church. Everyone is chattering happily, therefore I try to smile. I know it doesn't happen when my lips refuse to cooperate.

The wedding march starts. People return to their seats. Everyone hushes.

I watch the back of the church. The flower girls and ring boys come out first. They are all my temptress' nephews and nieces. I've been on my own most of my life, but the last two months, Winona's family became mine too. I've become an uncle, cousin, son and grandson.

Winona's bridesmaids, friends from school and college, follow. Then comes Ella, my temptress' best friend who's the maid of honor.

Finally, Winona comes into sight, accompanied by her father, and I breathe a sigh of relief.

She sees me. My heart settles.

Her eyes remain on my face as she strolls up the aisle, even when her father hands her to me, as if she knows how anxious I've been.

Throughout the ceremony, I can't stop feeling grateful. I never thought I'd find someone who gets me the way Winona does. I know I can be overpowering and demanding. There are times I want her all to myself. She understands.

It doesn't mean she takes all my craziness. She pushes back when she believes I'm crossing over a line she's not comfortable with. That's part of the reason I love. Because with her, I can be me without worrying I'll hurt or upset her. She's strong enough not to take any shit from me.

"Do you take this woman to be your lawfully wedded wife, forsaking all others, for as long as you both shall live?" The pastor asks.

"I do," I say, looking into Winona's champagne eyes.

When she affirms she takes me as her lawfully wedded husband, her voice is just as sure as mine.

We exchange the rings we commissioned together.

I put a lot of thought into the designs of these rings because they are a visual symbol that she's mine. Whenever she looks at the ring on her finger, I want Winona to think of the care I put into its design and know how much I love her. Know I'm the only man she's allowed to think about, just like she's the only woman on my mind.

"I pronounce you man and wife."

I take her into my arms and kiss her forehead. Then I kiss her mouth like a thirsty man, because for the last seven days, her family wouldn't allow us to be together. It was a tradition I wasn't very fond of.

Our guests go crazy, clapping, laughing and even whistling. The pastor clears his throat. Reluctantly, I tear my mouth away.

"Later, Lothario," Winona whispers against my ear.

"Yes, Temptress," I whisper back.

I can't wait to start my life with her.

The End

MARRYING THE BIG MOUNTAIN MAN

CURVY BRIDES OF BLOSSOM FORD #8

Keisha

AS THE MOUNTAINS of Blossom Ford, Arizona, come into view, my heart settles down a little. They look as breathtaking as they did in the photos Barret sent. I might be taking the greatest risk of my life, but at least I'll be doing it in a place that sings to my soul.

I signed up to Blossom Ford Matchmaking Agency's Mail-Order bride program on a whim, still, deciding to marry Barrett came from a place inside that connected with the type of person he is. My lips tilt up as I remember the words he used to introduce himself:

"I'm a big, callous ridden, rough around the edges man. Your life will be hard, but you'll have the satisfaction of knowing you've worked hard for your keep and the solace of being among nature's beauty. I can't give you sweet words, however you can expect a committed and hard-working man who'll provide for our family."

The words and their tone told me so much about my prospective husband.

He's offering what I'm searching for. A lasting marriage based on mutual trust, understanding and a will to make it work.

I've experienced first-hand the hurt and betrayal a passionate relationship brings and have decided to have nothing to do with it.

Mom and Dad were so happy in the early years of my life, I thought I was the luckiest girl alive. By the time I got to middle school, I stayed out as much as possible to avoid the arguing. They are the best of friends now, but before they divorced, my lovely parents had turned into two warring enemies.

Despite being jaded, I tried dating. I figured what I'd learned from seeing my parents fight and my desire and determination to have a healthy relationship gave me an advantage. It took forever to find a boyfriend. It turns out not many guys want to date a girl who's taller and bigger than them.

Eventually, I found someone who I thought might be the man of my dreams. It didn't last long.

"Baby, expecting me to sleep only with you is unreasonable. I thought you understood I'm a free guy. And I like variety," he'd said when I caught him cheating with a girl at least three times skinnier than me.

I hadn't understood. After that, I just couldn't bring myself to believe in passionate love. The pain of being in love didn't seem worth it to me.

Someone at work mentioned modern mail-order brides, horrified at the idea of a loveless marriage. The more I thought about it, the more sense it made sense. After I turned twenty-five and was made redundant for the second time in my life, I looked into it and came across Barrett's profile.

The train slows as it eases into Blossom Ford. I get up and gather my rucksack and suitcase. I'm about to open the door when it's wrenched back. A word of thanks is on the tip of my tongue when a huge hand reaches out and effortlessly lifts my suitcase down before I can reach it.

"Thank you," I say after I exit the train. I gaze up and up. It's an unusual thing for me. Being nearly six feet, I'm the person who usually looks down. He must be at least six feet four. A thrill runs through me. I'm such a sucker for tall men.

"Hi Keisha. I'm Barret."

His profile picture doesn't do him justice.

He's not a pretty man, yet I've met no one hotter. Thick, arched eyebrows frame his hazel eyes. A brown beard flanks lips meant to bring pleasure to a woman. Shoulder-length chestnut hair with blonde highlights reaches the top of his shoulders.

Heat flushes my cheeks. I realize I've ignored his outstretched hand while ogling him and flush again. I've always thought of my hands as huge, but my hand feels tiny in his much larger one.

All the chit chat I prepared vanishes from my mind, butterflies fill my tummy.

"It's nice to meet you," my voice is annoyingly croaky.

"You too. Let me take your rucksack."

"It's alright, I can carry it."

"You look like you can, but you've been traveling for hours. It's no trouble to me." He stretches his hand out like he won't accept no for an answer.

I'm so used to taking care of my own things, I'm ruffled for a moment. But then I remind myself I decided to embrace this new life.

I pass him the heavy bag and watch as he lugs it onto his back like it weighs nothing.

A whistle rings.

"Come on, the train is about to depart."

I follow Barrett down the platform, startled to notice I am the only person to get off the train.

There's a small parking lot outside with two trucks. Barrett leads me to the oldest one and as he stows my luggage in the trunk, I glance toward the sprawling town. Just breathing the air makes me feel good. I close my eyes and look up at the sky, luxuriating in the hot rays of the sun.

"Great, isn't it?"

My eyes fly open. Barrett is facing the mountains, admiration and pride emanating from his easy stance.

"I can feel the difference in air quality between here and Garnet City."

He goes to the passenger side and opens the door.

Something warm moves in my chest.

It's not just because I can't remember if any man has ever done that for me, it's the casual way he opens the door, like that's how he was brought up. It's so unlike his description of himself.

I get in the truck and watch as Barret closes the door and stalks around to the driver's seat. His height, burly chest and long legs as thick as tree trunks don't stop him from moving gracefully.

"Do you want to grab a quick bite before we head to the registry office?"

"I had a snack on the train."

I washed my face and freshened my makeup, too. Even though I am a cleanser and cream only girl, I plan on getting married only once; I want to look my best.

My ivory dress reaches just above my knees and shows my curves to what I hope is perfection. I had my hair pressed at the hairdressers yesterday and took great care to make sure it doesn't frizz. I swapped my heels for sneakers during my journey, but changed again when I freshened up.

"I was expecting more luggage," Barrett says as he heads away from the train station.

"Disappointed?"

"Hell no! If anything, I'm in awe."

"Clothes shopping is not a favorite. I keep a couple of nice dresses, but the rest of my clothes are jeans."

"I'm the same, so I'm glad to hear that."

"You have a couple of dresses too?"

Barrett chuckles. The sound is big and booming like him.

My heart skips a beat at the way his face transforms. He looks younger, more approachable.

As we drive through town, Barret points out places I might need to visit. He stops the truck after only a ten-minute ride outside an imposing building.

"We're here." He switches off the engine of the powerful car and faces me. "It's not too late to change your mind."

There's a steadiness in his voice that calms me. I'm surer now than when I left the city I grew up in.

"I'm sure."

I return his gaze, wanting him to see how determined I am.

When I responded to his request, he'd written back, saying I was too young to settle into the hard life of the mountain and he was too old for me. It took a lot to convince him my twenty-five years of age didn't diminish my desire for the type of life he was offering and that his age was a plus for me. I enjoyed living in the city, but I wouldn't miss it. I wanted a mature man who was ready to settle down, not a younger man not ready to be exclusive.

He nods and I sigh.

After he climbs out of the truck, I check my make-up one more time, reminding myself Barrett Montgomery is the man I decided to marry with a contract in order to build a strong marriage and a family. Passion doesn't come into it. Attraction is fine, it'll help things in the bedroom. However, falling in love is forbidden.

The success of this marriage is important to me. If I'm the only one who falls in love and Barret finds out, it might invalidate our contract. and that's something I don't want. So I tell my heart to stop being moved by his gentlemanly behavior and kindness.

MATCHED TO PATRICK

THE O'CONNORS OF BLOSSOM FORD #1

Patrick

MINGLED LAUGHTER DRIFTS from the sitting room, bringing mixed feelings of joy and sadness. We decorated the entire house in green–it's St Patrick's Day. As usual, we've been to church and are now having beef pot roast, which Mom and Aunt Shauna insist on making every year on the feast day of St. Patrick. Dad would have been so happy to hear that laughter. Even though we gathered like today at Christmas, St Patrick's Day was his favorite holiday.

I remove more salad from the refrigerator.

"Ready for the parade of women our moms no doubt have lined up for you this year?" My cousin Lorcan asks. I know his lilting voice like I know my own.

I snap the refrigerator closed. "Will I be the only one

on display?"

He winces. "You're the eldest. And you're Aunt Caitlin's only son, so you'll definitely be in the firing line. Mom will surely want to marry Riordan off first. I'll be an afterthought."

The lump in my throat prevents me from chuckling. I can't really blame Lorcan. I used to be like him. The thought of marriage drove me barmy. Not anymore.

At first I couldn't imagine myself being happy with a family, not with the crushing guilt I felt over what happened to Little Fiona. Before Dad passed, he made me promise to let go of that guilt and cherish the time I've been blessed with. Although I believed it'd never happen, little by little, I'm appreciating life.

I want what Mom and Dad had, though. They were meant for each other. Someone out there is my soulmate and the moment I find her, I'm not letting go. For the last couple of years, Mom and Aunt Shauna's matchmaking efforts haven't bothered me in the least.

I glance outside to where Riordan, my cousin and Lorcan's eldest brother, sits in the spring sun. "Riordan is not ready to get married. I doubt he'll hang around for the picnic and anyone our moms might want to set him up with."

That giant of a man is still blaming himself for what happened to his little sister Fiona, even though it's been twenty-six years since she was taken from us. Our dads were first cousins -both O'Connors. The two of us are forty-four, but I'm older than Riordan by one week. As the oldest children in the O'Connor family, it was our responsibility to make sure Fiona was safe.

Lorcan opens the back door.

"Mom is calling," he says to Rio.

It's the only thing that'll move my eldest cousin. Aunt Shauna may not be calling him now, but Riordan knows she'll soon be, wanting to make sure he spends as much time with us as possible before he scoots up the mountain.

Riordan and Lorcan's six brothers and Dad are watching TV while Mom and Aunt Shauna are chat.

"Don't forget to take good care of my friend Nara when she gets here. She was very kind to me the other day in town when I forgot my wallet," Mom reminds me.

We spend another couple of hours leisurely drinking and chatting, then get up to prepare for the outdoor picnic, which starts at four. The whole town is invited to our farm. Our parents started the tradition a few years after settling in Blossom Ford and starting a lettuce farm together, because they missed spending St Patrick's Day with their large family back in Ireland.

We put up tents on the large grass area between my house and Riordan's. Mom and Aunt Shauna used to do all the food when they were younger, but now, Lorcan gets caterers in to bring sandwiches and other finger food. By the time the townsfolk arrive, Cormac and Emmet, my youngest cousins, have set up a DJ stand which is playing upbeat music and the entire field is filled with green bunting and balloons.

I'm taking a breather from greeting people when I see a woman strolling towards Mom. Something about the way she walks catches my attention. She's wearing black skinny jeans that mold her curvy ass to perfection and a light green top that covers a pair of generous breasts and complements the sun-kissed tone of her skin. Wavy jet-black hair falls below her shoulders and shimmers in the sun.

I'm too far away to see the color of her eyes. Before I know it, I'm marching towards Mom, curiosity and something I can't name, compelling me forward.

"I'm so glad you came, Nara," Mom is saying when I reach her side on a strategic part of the field where she, Aunt Shauna, and their friend Ms. Penny can see everyone.

Tawny, that's the color of her eyes.

I answer myself as Nara greets everyone with an amiable smile that reaches her almond-shaped, yellow-brown eyes and warms the inside of my chest. She's comfortable around Mom, Aunt Shauna and their friends, even though she must be in her mid-twenties. The silver hoops on the tops of her ears glint in the sunshine.

"This is my son, Patrick." Mom points to me.

I stretch out my hand in greeting and when she holds mine; hers is small and smooth against my large and calloused one. I don't let go and she glances up at me.

That's when I know. That I've found the woman I've spent the last few years searching for.

The friendly warmth on her face is replaced by something else: interest. A tinge of pink fills her cheeks before she pulls her hand away.

Her voice cracks a little when she says hello leaving me to wonder where the confidence she exhibited a few moments ago went.

"I'll show you where the food is," I say.

"I don't want to trouble you." She looks about her. "I'll find it, thank you."

"It's no trouble at all," Mom beams at Nara. "Patrick will walk you over to the food area. Just ask him if there's anything you need to know."

A frown forms on my face as I lead the way. At my age, I'm old enough to know when a woman has the hots for me. I know Nara fancies me, but she's decided not to pursue it.

If there's one thing I'm good at, is getting to the root of a problem. Now I've found Nara, I'll have to convince her I'm the only man for her.

OTHER BOOKS BY THE AUTHOR

CURVY BRIDES OF BLOSSOM FORD SERIES

MARRYING THE PROTECTIVE PROFESSOR

MARRYING THE GRUMPY DIRECTOR

MARRYING THE POSSESSIVE NEIGHBOR

MARRYING THE WIDOWED DOCTOR

MARRYING THE SCARRED SOLDIER

MARRYING THE OBSESSIVE CEO

MARRYING THE BIG MOUNTAIN MAN

THE O'CONNORS OF BLOSSOM FORD SERIES

MATCHED TO PATRICK

ABOUT THE AUTHOR

Iris West writes short and spicy romance about alpha heroes and the women they can't help falling in love with. She loves reading all types of romance books that have a happy ending and is an avid Kdrama fan.

Follow or like her on Facebook and Goodreads.

FREE BOOK

Would you like a free book? Sign up to my mailing list at https://dl.bookfunnel.com/t191w45ryj to receive a copy of Loving My Fake Husband, a free to subscribers only, Curvy Brides of Blossom Ford Series short story.

HELP OTHERS FIND THIS BOOK

Thank you for reading Marrying The Obsessed CEO. If you enjoyed this book, please help others discover it by leaving a review at your favorite online book store.

Many thanks,

Iris xx

Milton Keynes UK
Ingram Content Group UK Ltd.
UKHW040903110923
428455UK00004B/256